This book belongs to:

. . . .

Also in the series:

The Fairies Arrive

THE FOREVER STREET FAIRIES: A CAKE FOR MISS WAND
by Hiawyn Oram and Mary Rees
British Library Cataloguing in Publication Data
A catalogue record of this book is available from
the British Library.

ISBN 0 340 84138 9

First edition published 2002
10 9 8 7 6 5 4 3 2

Published by Hodder Children's Books
a division of Hodder Headline Limited
338 Euston Road London NW1 3BH

Printed in Hong Kong

THE Forever Street Fairies

A Cake for Miss Wand

Written by

Hiawyn Oram

Illustrated by

Mary Rees

Hodder Children's Books

A division of Hodder Headline Limited

Contents

· · · · · · · · · ·

Chapter One

. . . .

Butterfly's Warning

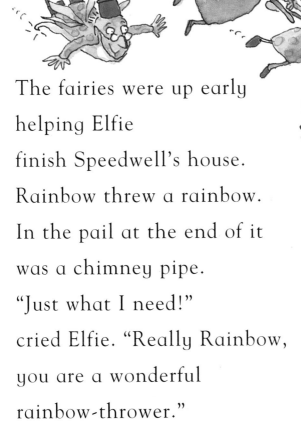

The fairies were up early
helping Elfie
finish Speedwell's house.
Rainbow threw a rainbow.
In the pail at the end of it
was a chimney pipe.
"Just what I need!"
cried Elfie. "Really Rainbow,
you are a wonderful
rainbow-thrower."

"And you are a wonderful
house-builder, Elfie,"
sighed Fingers.

"Thank you," said Elfie,
fixing the chimney pipe
to Speedwell's oven.

When it was done,
Speedwell rolled up her sleeves
and made a big batch of fairy cakes.
She arranged a picnic
on the mossy mound
under the oldest apple tree.

The fairies had hardly sat down
when up flew Bertie,
the big brown butterfly.
"Built all your houses then?"
he asked nosily.
"All except Elfie's," said Fingers.
"He's been so busy building ours,
he hasn't even started on his own."
"I see..." said Bertie,
helping himself to a fairy cake.

"Met Puffball, the poisonous
fairy yet?" he went on.
"Lives in a glass jar
just outside the gate.
Met the White Beast?"
"WHITE BEAST?" cried the fairies.

"Mmm, Cyclone the cat,"
said Bertie. "Belongs to Her.
The One Who Treads Softly.
She's been keeping him inside
since you arrived. But..."
There was a loud

PER-CLATTER.

Bertie got up to go.

"Ah... that's him now...

coming out of his little blue door.

Oh... and I do warn you,

he does hate anything that flutters!"

"Busybody," said Rainbow.

"Trying to frighten us..."

"Uh... maybe... or maybe not,"

said Elfie. "Look!"

Chapter Two

Cyclone Gets The Goblin

The fairies froze.

The White Beast was coming down

the path... looking this way...

looking that way...

sniffing...

pausing...

padding.

The fairies who could fly well,
flew into the tree.

Luckyday and Snip Snap

hid in the dandelions.

And the Beast kept on coming.

Close by
he stopped
and lay in the grass.
His eyes
were on the fluttering
in the tree.
Then he made his leap.
But he lost his footing,
turned in the air...

and landed
in the dandelions.

Snip Snap was a whisker away.
The Beast raised a paw...

and STRUCK!

Then, slowly, proudly,
he picked Snip Snap up
in his mouth
and slunk away.

Chapter Three

Cyclone Drops The Goblin

Miss Wand was sorting books
when she heard the cat flap clatter.
She saw the little grey bundle
in Cyclone's mouth
with its little red boots
and buttons and belt.
She knew what it was at once.

"DRO................P!"

she screamed.

"DRO...........P!"

Cyclone had never heard
Miss Wand raise her voice.

Now, here she was.

Not looking at him.

(She knew not to look
directly at fairies.)

Not coming at him.

(She knew not to get too close.)

Just mad and screaming,
"DROP THAT FAIRY
NOW AT ONCE!"

Cyclone was so surprised
he opened his mouth.
Snip Snap took his chance
and ran.
Cyclone's paw came after him.

But somehow
he found his wings
and rose... up... up...
out of reach
to a high shelf
and a dusty teapot
with the lid half off.
He went for the gap
tucked himself in
and did his best to...

KKFFFFFSHEW...

stifle a sneeze.

Chapter Four

Through The Small Blue Door

For two days Snip Snap hid
in the dusty teapot.
And for two days
the others worried.
Then they brought
their house-building ladders
and put them up
against the little blue door.

"I've been in there,"
said a bumble bee.
"And it was a mistake."
"And think of the Beast,"
said Bertie. "He could be
waiting for you
on the other side."
Rainbow flew up to
Miss Wand's kitchen window.

"It's all right," she reported back.
"The Beast's shut in."
So Luckyday and Elfie climbed the
ladder to hold the door open...
and one after the other
they all followed
and tumbled through
to the other side.

Chapter Five

A Treasure Trove For Fairies

"Snip Snap," they called softly,

"Mr Snip Snap...

Are you anywhere about?"

They heard a loud
KERCHOOO
and a louder

KERCHOOO!

A teapot lid smashed...
and Snip Snap appeared,
looking very dusty.

"And about
time too,"
he snapped.
"I'm STARVING!"

Fingers flew up
and helped him out.
"We were so worried!"
she cried.
"And I was so hungry!"
said Snip Snap. "I don't suppose
you brought me
anything to eat?"
"I'll see what I can do," said Rainbow.

She waved her wand
and threw a small dusty rainbow.
In the pail at the end of it
was half a dusty blackberry tart.
Snip Snap didn't care.
While he gobbled it up
the others looked round.

Even in the half-darkness,
they could see the shop
was a treasure trove.
They found
the dolls' house
and more furniture
like the furniture
Miss Wand had left them
the day they arrived.
"And look at these pots
and pans!" cried
Speedwell.
"And this washing
bowl and these
little stools!"
cried Fingers.

Then Elfie came upon his dream house.
It had lots of little windows
and steps leading up
to its own front door.
"If only..." he cried.
"But I'd never get it
out of here..."
He stopped.
They all froze.
Someone was coming.

With hearts fluttering
as hard as their wings,
they scrambled out
the way they'd come in.
But they needn't have been
afraid. It was only
Miss Wand on the landing,
not looking directly,
but knowing they were there.

Chapter Six

A Message From Miss Wand

"But how did it all get here?"
cried Elfie.
It was early the next morning
and the fairies had found
Elfie's dream house
in the long grass
by the old fish pond.

"And here are the pots and
pans I wanted!" cried Speedwell.
"And the washing bowl
and stools I wanted!"
cried Fingers.

"She must have put them here,"
said Luckyday.
"She Who Treads Softly."
"And left us the first furniture,"
said Fingers.

"And saved me from becoming
a cat's play-thing,"
said Snip Snap.
"Perhaps she's sending us
a message!" said the twins.

31

"That's just what she's doing,"
said Rainbow. "She's sending us
a message to say
she's a friend to fairies."
"Then we must send one back,"
said Elfie, "to say we'll be friends
to her. But what and how?"

Chapter Seven

A Giant Cake And A Little Dust

It was Speedwell who thought
of the giant fairy cake...
and Snip Snap
who thought of the dust.
"She likes dust," he said.
"We must sprinkle
the cake with it."
They worked through the day
and through the night.

Speedwell, Fingers, Nogo
and the twins mixed
the cake mix.
Elfie, Snip Snap
and Luckyday
hammered out
the baking tray.

Rainbow threw a rainbow
with a giant roll of
baking paper
in the pail.

Snip Snap
cut out
the baking cup.
And when the giant cake
was baked
they each sprinkled it
with a little of their own
fairy dust.

And, when Miss Wand came down
in the morning,
there it was
on the back doorstep.

She got the message at once
and carried it carefully into the shop.

"How I've waited for this!"
she cried.
"Waited for *what*, my dear?"
said her friend, the Count,
stepping in through the door.

Miss Wand cut the cake
in two and gave him half.
"Taste," she said.
"And you will see."

"Mmm! Mmm!" he cried, "so good
you'd think the fairies
baked it."

"That's just what I believe,"
said Miss Wand, as the Count
took her in his arms
and twirled her round the shop.

Then still going "Mmm!"
he danced out of the door
and down the street.

He didn't notice the fairy dust
on his cloak and shoes.
But Miss Wand
saw it fall
like a magic path.

She knew who had sent it.
And she wasn't surprised
that from that day on
no child passed her shop
without tugging and begging
to go inside – as if they now knew
just where to look for fairies!